To Rich

o yo

An accountant, always willing to help others. Keen in helping wildlife conservation and helping to fight cancer. Loves gardening, growing exotic plants, including orchids. Loves writing, dancing, Laugar Kung Fu, ancient history, various types of music and Entomology. Has various pets.

Best wishes

Chris. Hagi-Brown

11/11/2017

Dedication

To Layla, our female German Shepherd, who died on 24 September, 2015 and to Troy, Sasha, Zulu, Bam, Max, Sara, Heidi, Libby, Bramble, Kip, Honey, Tao and other pets.

Troy, you have been one great friend and soul mate to us all, a big softie, we all will miss you when you tilt your head when we talked to you, gave us your paw for friendship, those lovely hugs and licks, be at the front door to greet us.

To all of us who have known you it has been a pleasure, an honour to have known you, we will never forget you, our special and loveable friend. Be at peace, big boy, you are now reunited with Layla and all the animals in heaven.

Christopher Hayes Brown

LADY

AUSTIN MACAULEY PUBLISHERS™

LONDON • CAMBRIDGE • NEW YORK • SHARJAH

A CIP catalogue record for this title is available from the British Library.

ISBN 9781787107649 (Paperback)
ISBN 9781787107656 (E-Book)
www.austinmacauley.com

First Published (2017)
Austin Macauley Publishers Ltd.
25 Canada Square
Canary Wharf
London
E14 5LQ

Acknowledgements

To Mum, Dad, Nephew Oliver, Nan, Granddad Cook, Nan, Granddad Brown, Phyllis, Mollie, Mr and Mrs Harbour, Auntie Glenny, work colleagues, friends, fellow conservationists, etc.

In the two Great World Wars, many people gave up their lives for the sake of freedom, democracy and peace, with the hope that all nations will live in harmony with each other. There has been the cost and sacrifice of the many human lives that have been lost, whether they were friends, fathers, mothers, sons, daughters, brothers, sisters or other family relatives. We remember them in our hearts, and in our prayers.

But we must not forget those animals, remembering that we are all part of the animal kingdom, that also made the ultimate sacrifice. The horses, ponies, donkeys, dogs, pigeons, hawks, cats and the many other species of animals who also have played their part in those wars and given up their lives, so that we all could live in a better world. We should pay homage and pray for these special animals, and remember them for their unconditional love, kindness, courage, devotion to duty and, ultimately, the sacrifice of their lives in the name of freedom. They are the forgotten heroes.

This is one such story of an animal whose loyalty, courage, love and devotion touched the hearts of many people. One animal that we will never forget; especially not forgotten by one person named David Brown. The bond of friendship and for which love held no bounds, they both were totally devoted to each other, and they were true soulmates.

The story begins in January 1944, in a small peaceful Yorkshire village called Inkford. David Brown was a tall lanky lad with a mop of brown hair on his head and deep

9

blue eyes. He was the son of a farmer and enjoyed working on his father's farm. The name of the farm was Willow Tree, which has been owned by the Brown family for many generations; the name refers to the willow trees that grow along the banks of the stream that eventually runs into a small river travelling through some of the farmland.

The farm has about fifty acres of prime land, which is mainly used to grow various cereal crops, pastures for the dairy herds, and hay meadows for grazing by the sheep, goats and horses. There is also a large wood and wild flower meadow, a large orchard for growing of Bramley apples, Cox's eating apples, Conference pears, Opal, Victoria and Greengage plums, damsons, quince, sloes, as well as cob and hazelnuts. Adjoining the orchard are a variety of fruit bushes, including gooseberries, red, white and black currants, raspberries, strawberries, loganberries, tayberries. There are vegetables, various root crops, potatoes, various cabbages, and a plot for growing flowers, such as dahlias, sweet peas, chrysanthemums, etc.

The farm has a number of outbuildings, including stables, a dairy, large hay and straw barns, cereal barns, a barn for the overwintering of the livestock, a pigsty with grounds for the pigs to roam freely within, and a plot of land near the orchard for the chickens, ducks and geese to roam freely; there is also a large pond for the ducks and geese to paddle in.

The farm has a large back garden with a wildlife pond, and a large greenhouse for the growing of plants. There are herbaceous borders filled with various types of cottage plants, including cowslips, primroses, irises, geraniums, lupins, poppies, asters, delphiniums, ox-eye daisies, soapwort, various sunflowers, old-fashioned marigolds, violets, dead-nettles, violas, larkspur, sweet peas, sweet rocket, peonies, delphiniums, goldenrod, sedums, foxgloves, phlox, various shrubs including mahonia, elagans, mock orange, ribes, wintersweet, dwarf-pines, rhododendrons, shrub-honeysuckles and assorted rocky plants in an odd ceramic sink. There are various types of herbs such as mint, rosemary, lavenders, thymes, sage, parsley, old-fashioned scented roses, honeysuckles, jasmines and a Japanese blue flowering wisteria growing along the side of the farmhouse.

The other side of the farm is open woodland with a mix of beech, oak, holly, privet, pines, ash, willow, birch, dog-roses, rowan, sloe, etc. In the spring, the forest floor is carpeted in wood anemones; in summer, it is full of bluebells, cowslips, and primroses; and in late summer, it is then full of foxgloves.

The farmhouse is furnished in various pine, elm and oak furniture. There are dressers, chesterfield furniture, velvet curtains, old grandfather clocks in the hall and the sitting room, cast iron beds with handmade quilted covers, copper pans, pots, etc. There are sheepskin rugs throughout the house, lead-lighted windows, a fire in the sitting room and kitchen, and the kettle always on the boil. The property was so inviting and welcoming to any visitor who may pass to visit the Brown family.

David was doing his early morning rounds on the farm; checking that the animals are all in good health, fed, the cows are milked, and also collecting the eggs from the hens.

On his way back to the farmhouse, his father shouted to him, "Breakfast is on the table, David." He entered the kitchen to the warmth coming from the open log fire, the smell of freshly baked bread, steaming hot tea, and his family all around the kitchen table.

"Happy birthday, David," they all said joyfully; then next was the handing out of the presents. His mother gave him a kiss and presented him with a pair of knitted socks and a scarf, his two younger brothers, Oliver and Sam, gave him a bag of sweets, and then finally, his father turned to him.

"Happy birthday, son," he said, then opened the side door to reveal a six-month-old medium haired puppy with fluffy ears, long lanky legs, and those lovely puppy dog eyes that would melt the hearts of many a person. She was the most beautiful black-and-tan female German Shepherd, sitting in her basket, wagging her long bushy tail and, with those brown eyes, looking at David; she was listening to every word and titling her head from side to side.

David was so overwhelmed with the surprise.

"Well, son, do you like her, and what are you going to call her?" his father said.

He replied, "Lady, that is what I will call her," and with that he walked towards her and stroked her head. "Well, Lady, it seems we are going to be good friends."

Lady looked, staring at him, and tilted her head and then presented him with her paw. "You are an intelligent, loving, and affectionate dog, Lady, and it looks we are going to get on fine," he said.

David then headed back to the table to have breakfast with the family. He sat down and started tucking into a well-deserved breakfast of hot buttered toast, scrambled eggs, fried bacon and tomatoes, and a large mug of tea when the next thing he felt was a paw on his leg.

"Well, Lady, it seems you are hungry too." And Lady sat looking up to David with those *butter would not melt* eyes.

He presented her with a slice of bacon, which she gently took from him, then laid down to tuck into it.

His mother then turned around to Lady. "Where are my manners, you must be hungry too? Dad, pass me a plate I will put a couple of slices of bacon and a sausage on it." And she then placed the plate on the floor for Lady to eat. "There, that will set you up for the morning until dinner time," said David's mother.

Then David got up after finishing breakfast, saying, "Well, Lady. I will go up and check the sheep on the hill now, Dad, and then I will check the cattle in the pastures," then headed to the door followed by Lady.

His father then said, "Okay, son, we'll see you later. I nearly forgot, here is Lady's collar and lead to put on her."

"Thanks, Dad", said David. David then got Lady to sit, while he put on her new collar and lead.

Dad then said, "I will take your two brothers to check on the new Iron Age and Leicester Old Spot piglets that have just been born early this morning in the pig enclosures."

As David was walking towards the hill, he felt within him a presence that a strong bond would be forged between him and Lady, and that they would never leave each other's side; to be soulmates. There was also a feeling of an unconditional love and devotion to each other, a true bond between man and dog he had never felt before.

Lady was a very inquisitive dog, and loved to play all the time whether with David and/or with his family. She loved playing with the old cricket ball and particularly became attached to and loved carrying David's brown, well-worn and once-loved old teddy bear. At night, she would sleep on David's bed and cuddle the teddy bear, which she had now adopted as her own toy. Sometimes she would even sneak under the blankets, dragging the teddy bear with her when the nights were cold, and then cuddle up to David, clutching her teddy bear.

Over the period of time, Lady had truly become part of the family; they loved her and she loved them, particularly David.

Well, the months rolled on since David's eighteenth birthday, and Lady had grown from a young puppy into a very handsome young dog, and the bond between them had also grown stronger and stronger. Wherever David went, Lady would follow, whether it be up the hillsides, walks down the beautiful country lanes, or rounding up the large herd of Guernsey and highland cattle and the fifteen sheep, which now had new lambs in a paddock next to the farm barn, to helping mucking out the farm animals if she was not rolling in it. Also to watch the feeding of the various farm animals, including the four Shire horses, the milking of the Guernsey goats and the cattle.

There were four tabby-marked farm cats to help keep the rat and mice population down. Lady was unsure of them, particularly as they had some powerful sets of claws, which did get in the way of her nose from time to time. She also became amused with the various breeds of chickens, geese and the ducks; sometimes, she would get pecked at for being too nosey, which would make her yelp and run to David with her tail between her legs.

Lady was always curious over the frogs and toads in the garden pond because of the croaking sounds they made, particularly in the springtime, and many a time she would fall into the pond. She was also very intrigued with the Aylesbury ducks with their waddle when they walked and the noise they made.

Curiosity was Lady's middle name, always interested in what was going on in the farm and in the garden. One thing she did love was to swim in the nearby stream.

Lady was also very much adored by the villagers, particularly when visiting the greengrocer, the baker, the post office staff, the local police, and passing the local pub with the smell of the home-cooked pies, cheese macaroni, roast dinners, etc. The pub was aptly named the 'Dog and Duck', and had a warm log fire to welcome guests with the local ales and cider. One thing Lady always looked forward was, of course, seeing the children in the local school. Lady loved being made a fuss of and, as always, gave back that love to the villagers and their children.

On one sad occasion, the David family went over to visit Mr and Mrs Claydon. The youngest of the children, Master James, had developed a very bad chest infection over the past few months, which unfortunately seemed to be getting worse, despite the various medications prescribed to help combat the infection. While Mum and Dad would sit and chat to the Mr and Mrs Claydon, trying to comfort them both, David and his brothers, accompanied by Lady, went to see James in the sitting room, all wrapped up in a thick blanket by a log fire to help and try and keep him warm, while his brother and sister would play with their toys on a large woollen rug.

David went over to James and then said, "Look who has come to see you, James." With that, Lady went up to the boy, rubbing her head against him, inviting him to stroke her. David felt so sorry for James; he was so pale and very weak from trying to fight off the infection. Over the next couple of days, David would make regular visits with Lady to see James, but he was not getting any better and, at times, James would cough up small amount of blood. All his family could do was to give him the medication and try and keep him comfortable.

Then one cold and frosty morning, David and Lady arrived at the Claydon's house to find the family in tears. David and Lady headed to James's bedroom to see a priest administering the last rites; James lay there coughing, so pale and very thin. David sat next to James and held his hand which was so cold to touch. Lady then hopped straight onto his bed and nestled up to him, and James then tried to stroke Lady with tears in his eyes. The family were then beckoned to enter the room to say their last goodbyes to James by Father O'Ryan. Then within minutes, James fell into a deep sleep, holding onto Lady. It was so emotional. David got up and moved to the door with Lady, paying his last respects to the family. Then he said, "I will let Mum and Dad know and ask them to visit you all, I am so sorry." With that he shut the door and walked off up the hill to the farm, tears rolling down his eyes, Lady stayed close to him all the time looking up to him.

The funeral was well-attended by the people from the village and surrounding villages, and the school children sang the song 'Never Ending Love', which was so emotionally received by all. At the end of the funeral, Mr Claydon then got up to sing 'Edelweiss' and was joined by the church choir. It truly touched the souls of everybody in the church. Then the coffin was carried outside to where James was to be buried near a yew tree, and with the view looking down towards the village. His headstone had a carving of a dove holding a sprig of holly, and the words of the headstone read:

'To our darling James who we all miss so much, and is now in the arms of God and his angels. God bless and rest in peace our wonderful son and brother.'

James Claydon was missed by the whole village. A sad loss of such a young life.

Thereafter life seemed so peaceful on the farm for David and Lady for a short period of time, but their world was going to change for both of them. As more and more people were being drafted up to join the various armed services to help in the war effort, it would only be a matter of time before David would be called up. David was concerned that when he was called up, he would have to leave Lady behind. This played on his mind and worried him a lot. David was more than happy to serve his king and country, but his heart would break if he had to leave Lady; she had become such a main part of his life now.

Then one day, David had just come in from outside after checking that the cattle in the fields were all right, ready to have his dinner with Lady, when he was greeted by sad faces from his family. His mother had tears in her eyes, and his brother ran over to hug David and make a fuss of Lady.

His father turned to David in a choked voice, trying not to get too emotional. "Son, we have received some sad news, a letter from the War Office. It is your call-up papers, and you are required to register at the local army barracks."

David's face sank with sorrow knowing that day had come, and Lady's ears moved back, her look of sadness in those brown eyes, David turned towards Lady and bent down to cuddle her. "It seems I must leave you." She then gave him her paw. Breaking down in tears, he held her close to his face. David said, "I so love you, Lady, and will miss you and my family, but I have a duty to now serve my country."

With that his father said, "David, that may not be the case, as the army is also recruiting men to volunteer to carry out patrols with guard dogs while on active service, like day and night patrols around the campsites."

David turned to his dad. "Do you really think that there could be a chance for Lady and me to serve together in the army?

His father said, "Well there is only one way to find out."

David said, "That would be great for us both to be together, but we are really going to miss all of you."

David's mum then said, "Now, now, you will soon be back home before you know it."

His father then said, "We need to register you as soon as possible, and also to find out if Lady can be registered as a guard dog. You both have such a bond with each other which may well be to your advantage and, of course, this would also help you both through your period of active service in the army. God willing, you both will come back safely from the war and back to us here on the farm.

Then they all hugged each other. David's dad turned to David and said, "Son, we are going to miss you both so much." And then he bent down to cuddle Lady. "Especially you."

Well, the day finally arrived for both of them. The army registration went well for David, he passed his medical, and Lady was accepted as a patrol dog after vigorous training. The training was tough in those few weeks for both of them, but they kept their spirits up as they had each other, and the friends they made at the camp.

Lady in particular was much-loved by David's comrades, the NCOs, the captain and his good wife, who would spend some time with Lady while David was undertaking the vigorous training such as rifle shooting, armed and unarmed combat, physical training, map reading and night patrols, in preparation for active service.

On his one and only short leave from the army before going to war, David would spend as much time as he could alone with Lady, building that bond with her, up on the Yorkshire hills, and also helping with the farm animals and spending quality time with his family.

Then, on the last day after their training, the now newly-trained recruits decide to go skinny dipping in the lake at the back of the camp. Lady, as usual, joined in, enjoying doggy-paddling about in the water. All of a sudden, from behind a clump of trees appeared the captain and his wife on their afternoon stroll. The captain said, "Well men, stand and salute your commanding officer."

David turned and said, "We cannot, we are all naked, Captain, and we do not want to embarrass your good wife." All of the lads remained in the water only showing the top half of their body, while Lady was excitedly swimming around them all.

The captain's wife turned to them and said, "Boys will be boys. Let them enjoy the rest of their spare time. Now let them be, my husband." She then smiled at them. With that, they, the captain and his wife, walked off into the distance.

David and his comrades got out of the water to get dried and dressed, then David got his towel to dry Lady, and said, "With your thick coat, you are like a sponge absorbing all this water, it will take me a while to dry you off." Then the lads and Lady finally marched off back to the barracks singing 'We'll Meet Again'.

The day came for the new recruits' passing out parade, which was a special day for all, in particular the parents who watched their sons marching in their new uniforms and Lady walking to heel by David's side.

A very proud day for all. After the parade was finally dismissed, they all went over to the mess to have a bite to eat and to chat, while Lady's interest was, of course, the lovely food laid out on the table. And, as usual, Lady was spoilt by having a dish of cold meats, washed down with a bowl of cold water.

David knew soon the time would come for them to be travelling abroad, into unknown territories. Also unknown to them was what may lie ahead for both of them, so now they both had to be prepared and keep their spirits up, and try to enjoy themselves.

That day finally came for David to leave the farm with Lady. It was a warm, sunny day, and the spring flowers were out in the garden. David was smartly dressed in his army uniform, carrying his kitbag, into which, unbeknown to him, Lady had sneaked her teddy bear. Lady was well groomed and wearing her army-issued brown leather collar with the number 33 stamped on it; she was now officially in the service of the army, the king, and their country. His mother, early that morning, had given David a medallion of St Christopher to wear around his neck, which he duly did. It was a very sad day for the family as they prepared for David and Lady to leave the family home.

The family walked down together to the bottom of the farm lane, there to be greeted by a small detachment of soldiers in readiness to march down to the local railway station. The family said their farewells with tears in their eyes, hugging and kissing David and Lady. For the family to say their goodbyes, it was heartbreaking and very emotional for all.

"Come back safely, both of you," said his father.

David then turned to his father, "Yes, we will."

Lady replied with a bark and with that David waved to his family as he walked off with Lady by his side.

The family then watched very emotionally as David and Lady marched on their way with the rest of the soldiers heading towards the train station, singing, as they marched, 'It's a Long Way to Tipperary' with all the passion within their souls.

David's father turned to the rest of the family and said, "God bless them both. God protect them and bring them both back home safely to us." And he knew for now that the farm would not be same again without them.

His mum then turned, hugged David's dad saying, "We must be brave for them and try to keep all our spirits up until they both return. How long, only time will tell." She then said, "Almighty God, protect them both, and please also send a guardian angel to watch over them both and their fellow comrades."

Well, as they marched down the narrow road, a good five miles' hike, towards the railway station, the soldiers then started to sing 'There'll be bluebirds over the white cliffs of Dover', and Lady wagged her tail from side to side in response.

As they passed through the village, David noticed that the villagers had turned out to cheer them on. "Good luck to our brave boys," shouted the villagers, and then the school children started waving their Union Jacks, and cheering the soldiers on.

Then the village shopkeeper approached the soldiers and presented them with sandwiches made from freshly-baked bread with various fillings, including cheddar cheese and slices of ham, and also some with various homemade jams. The soldiers were also given a large bag of eating apples from the grocer's orchard and various fruit cordials, bottles of mineral water from the local hillside spring, and the butcher then gave a juicy knuckle bone, all wrapped to David, for Lady to enjoy on the train.

Next, two spinsters, Betty and Penny from Wisteria Cottage, came over to give the soldiers some of their freshly-baked fruitcakes filled with a rich, creamy butter filling. Then they both said, "Don't forget, David, to let Lady have a piece of the cake, you know how much she loves it." With that they gave David hugs and kisses and they then made a fuss of Lady, before they walked back towards the cottage, wiping the tears from their eyes.

The baker then said to the soldiers, "The food and drink is for your journey, you brave lads. God bless you all, and come back safely." The villages then joined in cheering the soldiers. The soldiers thanked all of the villagers for their kindness and then they started to march on towards the railway station.

Upon finally arriving at the railway station, they then embarked onto the train in an orderly fashion. Some of the other villagers had now arrived, and also the local farmers, to help wave them off as the train left the platform. The soldiers waved back from their carriage windows, and then they finally sat down in their carriage to tuck into some of the food that the villagers had kindly given them, for it would be some time before they would have their next meal.

Lady lied down by David. He then broke off a piece of fruit cake for Lady to eat, which went down a treat. She then licked the crumbs off the carriage floor before finally starting to chew on her bone for the rest of the train journey. David started to eat a ham sandwich, then a piece of fruitcake, followed by some diluted bramble cordial, which did round the meal off a treat.

Their journey was long and took them several hours before they reached Dover Railway Station. While on their journey, they passed several picturesque villages, some towns, a few rivers and such wonderful landscapes that it did bring home to them what they both would be missing and leaving behind. But David knew in his heart that these lands, which are so special as are its people, the animal and plant life, above all this wonderful country, is what they would be fighting for. For the freedom, the peace, for democracy, for a better world and to help put an end to the cruelty of the Nazi regime.

Lady enjoyed chewing her bone until finally there were only small pieces left, she then, after having enough, eventually started to settle down next to David and fell asleep. The other soldiers in the compartment, full from consuming the delicious food and drink, also took the opportunity to have a sleep before they would finally arrive at Dover.

Eventually, they arrived at their destination at Dover Railway Station, all tired from the very long journey. They all got up and started to disembark off the train in an orderly fashion, to the smell of the fresh sea breeze, and they then started to march in an orderly fashion towards the awaiting troopships ahead at the harbour, only to be met by other soldiers from various garrisons. The soldiers finally stopped in an orderly fashion next to their respective drill sergeants so that the local priest could say Mass. Then the soldiers started to sing 'Onward, Christian Soldiers' in full voice, following which the priest gave his blessing to them all. The drill sergeants then gave the order for the soldiers to embark onto their own troopship.

Once on aboard, David, Lady and their fellow comrades were asked to stand to attention, while their senior commanding officer, Major Edwards, stepped forward to address them. "Men," he said. "Once we have finally disembarked from the troopship, we will be travelling by truck to Paris, and then from there, you will be split up into smaller units to help to take out any German patrols left behind from the last few nights' raids. Finally, you will be sent to your location somewhere on the edge of Germany. This will be told to you nearer the time; for now, your respective unit commander will have the maps so that they can guide you all thorough the various terrains. God willing, you will eventually meet up with other British troops, so that a combined fighting force can be formed to fight off the retreating Germans. Now, be aware, men, at any point those Germans may spring some surprises on you, so be on your guard at all times. Now, finally, men, get some rest, we will be landing on the Normandy beaches early tomorrow morning, good night, and good luck. God bless you all."

They then stood to attention and saluted the Major before he left.

While on the ship, Lady remained constantly by David's side, looking for reassurance from him. He gently stroked her on the head. "Now, Lady, we have a big day tomorrow," said David.

Lady's eyes looked up to him. "There, there, I will always be with you, and protect you; you are so special to me, Lady," said David in a soft voice.

Lady then gave her paw to him, next thing she decided to play with other soldiers, a game of throwing the ball to and fro between Lady and the soldiers. This went on for a quite a while, which helped to relax the soldiers by keeping their minds off the war and, of course, kept Lady entertained. It was great to see the soldiers also laughing and in high spirit, and Lady, as usual, the centre of attention and she loved every minute of it.

Eventually, Lady started to get tired of the game, so she then went over to one of the soldiers, starting to gently tug at his cap. She then rolled over onto her back and allowed him to tickle her belly, then finally, with all of the excitement, she went back tired and exhausted to lay down by David, putting her head on his lap and then fell asleep.

David sat stroking Lady, deep in thought as to what was going to happen to them when they land in France, concerned about their fate, knowing that they have a duty to serve their country, that they are now in hands of God, and praying that all of them will arrive safely back in England again.

Eventually, in the early hours of the morning, the ships arrived at their destination, the Normandy Beach, the troops started to disembark from the troopships, then they had to cautiously cross the beach listening to the sound of gunfire, but all they could see was smoke arising from a town in the distance that had not long been bombed by the retreating German soldiers. While David marched with Lady, he was amazed by the sights he saw in a makeshift hospital, where some of the soldiers were being treated for their horrific wounds from the previous conflict with the Germans.

It was indeed a nerve-racking sight indeed, seeing dead and decaying bodies of young and old men, some with parts of their body missing, some a mix of legs, arms and torsos piled up in a corner, ready to be taken to the incinerators by some of the nursing staff. For the new recruits, this must have been a frightening sight to see, the horrors of war.

Lady did not show any fear, but gave courage to help them move on, and I think this gave encouragement and reassurance to David and his comrades as they finally embarked onto the army trucks waiting along the roadside for them, to take them on the long and somewhat dangerous journey through France.

While travelling, Lady, as usual, tried to keep everyone's spirits up by brushing up to the soldiers, egging them on to stroke her. David said, "Oh Lady, I am so glad you are with us, such innocence and devotion you show to us all."

While on their travels, they saw many sights that could turn a strong person's stomach over. Burnt out buildings, inhabitants looking dismayed and in despair as what was once their home had now gone. Some dead bodies littered about the ground to be collected and then carried away for burial. And the stench of death, the children staring in horror in their torn clothes, some children were even clutching onto whatever they could get hold for reassurance. A priest giving the last rites to some unfortunate soul, some women crying and putting their hands out to us. A father weeping as he carries his legless son's body with blood still pouring from the boy's wounds, and also so many people begging for food and some trying to find food amongst the rubble. It was so pitiful. This touched David's soul, and at one point, his eyes welled up with emotion from the sights he saw.

Then travelling on, they passed many towns, villages, farmlands, woods and forests bombed and destroyed on a massive scale. None of these places had been spared the mercy of the retreating German army.

Hours finally passed when they finally reached the edge of Paris, which was also badly war-torn. The soldiers disembarked from the trucks, formed into their own units and then moved off on foot going their separate way, and eventually onto their final destination: into Germany.

While David's own unit marched on, they came across further sights of dismay, tearful, soul searching, and the horror of what the war had done to these homeless people, battered from the war and starving. A little girl clutching her headless doll for comfort, dogs and cats searching for food amongst the rubble, buildings fully or partly blown up, burnt public and military vehicles, vegetation destroyed, trees burnt down, there was no sound of the birds singing or in flight, and the smell of death around them. Dead bodies being carried away and put onto horse drawn carts, and smoke in the air, further sounds of shelling from guns firing in the distance. Then the next thing they could hear was people singing in a small church a few yards away from them. One could only hope the consolation, safety, sanctuary and prayers were keeping the poor souls' spirits up. It is times like this you do look to your faith for hope, guidance and spiritual peace.

They kept marching on and now keeping close to the forests ahead for cover and always staying away from any main roads for fear of being easy targets for any German planes in the air, and also from being spotted by any retreating German convoys. One of their main objectives was to surprise and then disable any German patrols they come across, but fortunately, they had been blessed so far. They had seen enough killings so far.

The days and nights were long and tiring as they marched on, but with their strength, their willpower and keenness to reach their final destination, and with the knowledge that they would bring help and relief to the troops already in Germany. Lady, as usual, kept up with the rest of the unit and always stayed close to David, ears alert for any unusual sounds or noises.

During that time, David and Lady remained a constant source of strength to each other, and also a reminder to each other of their happy times back home on the farm. She was a joy and comfort not just to David but also to the rest of the soldiers, and I think that's what kept them going and pushing them on towards Germany.

During their travelling, they only stopped for rest and for food, but only at night times and in the safety of the woods or the forests, always careful that any fires lighted could not be seen, and in the early hours of the morning, they cleared any evidence that they had ever been there.

It was one cold, wet, misty morning when all of a sudden there came the firing of guns from a distance, with also the occasional burst of shell fire. They knew they were not that far from the German frontline now, where all the action was taking place.

They continued marching down along a muddy track carved through what seemed a very large pine forest. Then, all of a sudden, a burst of gunfire came from within the forest. The captain turned and quietly beckoned them all to take cover to prevent them all from being ambushed out in the open, so they did, their guns ready to fend off any enemies within.

David, shaking with nerves from the ordeal, was gentle nudged by Lady, reminding him she was near him. They took cover behind some thick bushes, his hearts beating fast, his gun loaded and ready to fire at any advancing German soldiers. David waited for the Captain's order. The gunfire became louder and louder, and then all of a sudden, the gunfire stopped and everything became quiet. David eventually decided to move cautiously with his gun held in his hand, ready to fire away from the bushes, but only to find to his horror his captain and some of his comrades lying dead on the ground, full of gunshot wounds, some to the head and chest. He walked further along the road to see some men barely alive, some were lying on the ground, some wriggling with pain and agony from their gunshot wounds; it was a bloody mess. With David's heart pounding with fear, he decided to pluck up the courage to help his injured comrades and to dress their wounds the best he could from the medical bag he was carrying, and also to comfort them as best he could.

He noticed that he was the only soldier so standing, and now alone with his wounded companions for company.

Lady, as always, was making a fuss of the wounded, even offering them her paw to show a form of comfort and reassurance to the injured men.

Then, all of a sudden, a gun fired from within the forest, and David fell to the ground.

When David finally woke up, in pain from his injury and blood running down the side of his face, he looked up towards the sky only to see two young German soldiers looking down at him.

One of them then said, "Well, this one is still alive." David looked up to them and the first thing in his mind was Lady. His hand moved to his side to feel that Lady was lying next to him, with her head on his chest. One of the German soldiers turned to him and said then, "Who is this?"

David said in a muffled voice, "My name is David and this is my faithful dog, her name is Lady."

She then sat up and tilted her head to catch the sounds of the spoken voices and then gave one of the soldiers her paw. "Hello, Lady," he said. "Nice to meet you," and held her paw gently. "You remind me of my German Shepherd back home, his name is Bruno."

Then two German soldiers started to help David onto his feet. He still felt dizzy and in pain, but he at least managed to walk with Lady by his side, towards an army truck parked at the side of the forest. A soldier got out and opened the back of the truck. Then one of the German soldiers turned to David and said, "We will help you, Lady, and your injured men into the truck, and then we will be off to Stalag 14, a prison camp near the Austrian border, and there you will all remain until the end of the war."

Their journey took them through many towns and villages. David noticed a small German force, made up of a few soldiers on foot, some battered tanks, trucks and armoured personnel carriers pass them by.

Eventually, they arrived at Stalag 14, a very large enclosed prison surrounded with barbed wire fencing, several control towers supported with spot lights, and soldiers manning the machine guns. Also various buildings within, trucks, and then a secondary internal barbed wire fence surrounded a number of huts within the campsite, and a number of German soldiers on patrol with their dogs.

Upon entering the main gate to the compound, they were greeted by the cheers and sounds of the prisoners, who were held back by a number of German soldiers to stop them going too close to the truck.

They finally disembarked from the truck and were helped by their fellow inmates off towards the hospital, there to have their wounds treated, cleaned and dressed. Lady, as always, was by David's side; the German soldiers watching them seemed not to be worried about this; in fact, they enjoyed making such a fuss of her as she headed into the hospital.

To the Germans, it was probably usual to capture soldiers who also had a dog with them; however, they did notice that Lady was the property of the British army, as one of the soldiers noticed that there was a number on her collar with the local regiment's coat of arms embossed on the collar.

David sat on a bed while his head wound was cleaned and dressed by a medic; Lady sat by him looking attentively, David gently stroked her head as reassurance.

He could hear the sounds of some of his comrades in agony from their wounds, one soldier had to be put to sleep so as his left leg could be amputated, another soldier had his badly damaged arm strapped up as best as the medic could do. There must have been about fifteen of them injured in the hospital, and the few doctors with their medics were doing what they could to comfort them all.

Then those that had been treated and could walk were then taken outside of the hospital to be given instructions by a British corporal, Jack Holland, who addressed them on how to behave while in the camp. Lady sat and listened by David's side.

Then the sergeant, Andy McAllister, stepped forward and started to allocate them to the appropriate huts. Thankfully for David and Lady, they were assigned to hut four with some of his own comrades. As they marched over to the hut, some of the Germans soldiers stood and watched their every movement and also looked out for anything suspicious on them. Once they arrived inside the hut, they were greeted by their fellow comrades, who would be sharing the hut with them over the period of their imprisonment.

David and Lady felt welcomed, and some of the men came over to make a fuss of Lady. It was a long time since many had seen a friendly dog and a very affectionate one, and soon Lady started to befriend them all. One inmate bent down to Lady, hugging her with tears in his eyes; it was so emotional.

David turned and said, "This is Lady." Lady then held her paw out to the soldier who then held it gently and she also gave him a lick on the face.

"Well, hello, Lady, my name is Max," he said. "The only animals that we ever see are the German Shepherd dogs with the German soldiers patrolling around the prison camp perimeter. However, we do see the occasional bird flying down to feed off our homemade bird table outside, but that is the only other wildlife we do see here," said Max.

During that evening, the fellow inmates spent their time discussing their adventures, their home lives, friends, family, and David spent some time talking about his life back at the farm with Lady. Finally, he said good night to them all. Then, David went to his bunk bed, exhausted from the long day and fell straight onto the bed while Lady went to the rucksack and pulled out her teddy bear, hopped onto the bed next to David where she then curled up next to him and cuddled her teddy bear. David put his arms around Lady tightly with tears from his eyes rolling down his face. She nuzzled into him to comfort him, and then they finally fell asleep.

Next morning, all the inmates got up to wash and get dressed, when suddenly they heard whistles being blown and shouting from outside, and then several German soldiers came into the hut.

"Roll call! Roll call!" shouted the German officer.

They then all had to march out of their hut onto the parade ground, standing to attention, while a German officer gave the roll call to the British contingent, calling out their names, to which the inmates responded in turn. Lady sat to attention. When the German officer called out number 33, Lady tilted her head, and then barked in response. He then repeated the process with the American, French, Polish and the other contingents.

Then a group of senior German officers appeared and started to move towards David's group. One of the senior German officers stepped forward. "Well, who is this young dog?" Lady looked up at him, wagging her tail with excitement.

David then said, "This is Lady."

"Well," said the officer, "hello, Lady." He bent down, to be greeted by her offering her paw to him. He shook it gently and then stroked her on the head, and commented, "I hope all of you men will be as well behaved as this young dog." He then turned and walked away with his fellow officers to the Polish contingent.

Once the parade ended, they all headed off towards the large hut to get their breakfast; a mixture of a thick porridge, some dried bread and a mug of stewed tea. They all started to eat heartily as it had been a long time since they had eaten. Lady was allowed a bowl of porridge mixed with some milk, which she lapped up eagerly. David then said, "Well, Lady, you were hungry too." She turned and barked.

Once they had finished breakfast, they all went outside to spend the time either playing sports such as football or reading what books there were on the bookstand. Some the inmates went walking around the camp to pass the time while others stood chatting. David and Lady decided to walk around together, surveying their new home, knowing that until such a time when they may leave, they must accept this was their home for the duration of the war.

Then late afternoon, they all filed back into the large hut to have their evening meal, which was a type of thick vegetable stew with a small amount of meat, some dried bread and a mug of water.

Lady was given a bowl of stew, but was given a bit more meat; again she lapped it up.

Then, once finished, all got up to spend a bit of time outside, before the German soldiers would ask them to return to their huts for the night until the following morning.

Once they were in their hut, some of the inmates would sit and play cards, others would lay on their beds to read their letters, some would sit and chat together. As for David and Lady, she would play catch the ball with some of the men, then finally the lights were turned off and they all then went to their beds.

This became the standard ritual for them all, day in and day out.

Over a period of time, David and Lady got to know their fellow inmates very well, and Lady was always a centre of attention. One of her jobs was to visit the sick men in hospital, to comfort them, and to give them a sense of hope to their lives.

David loved spending many a happy hour growing flowers and vegetables from seeds given to him by one of the German officers. These were germinated on the hut windowsills. David also spent some time training a scented pale, pink rambling rose to trail over an arch next to the plot. The vegetables grown were various types of cabbage, swedes, carrots, leeks and onions. Occasionally, he managed to grow some potatoes from sprouting tubers, given to him by the kitchen staff, on the small plot of land. The vegetables were used for thick soups, stews if lucky, with homemade dumplings and vegetable roasts with batter puddings when there were spare eggs from the chickens.

They lived in a homemade chicken house with run, which David enjoyed building. Lady would sit and watch the hens strutting about, pecking at the vegetable waste and a bit of corn. The chickens were donated to them by a local farmer in return for helping to make fencing for his livestock. The flowers grown were planted around the rose arch to give added colour and some scent. David was also given some alpine strawberries to grow in pots. The fruit were small but gave a little change to their normal diet.

A couple of weeks had passed when there was the arrival of a couple of trucks with a German officer's staff car escorted by several soldiers on motorbikes. The small convoy of vehicles started to make its way into the inner camp compound itself. The inmates all started to move towards the vehicles, only to be held back by the camp's guards. Next thing, the camp commandant appeared with several of his officers who were moving towards the staff car, only to be greeted by several SS officers. Next, filing out of one truck were several soldiers all lined up to attention, and then out of the second truck appeared some more soldiers escorting two prisoners who were handcuffed. The next thing they heard was a very heated conversation between a senior SS officer and the camp commandant, then silence filled the camp, Lady nuzzled up close to me for comfort. They all froze with fear as they all had heard about the terrible things the SS got up to. And none of them were ever good.

The next thing they saw was the two prisoners were made to stand against one of the hut walls. Six SS soldiers lined up facing them, followed by one of the officers. The soldiers were then told to take aim, and the officer shouted fire. The two prisoners fell to the ground, then dead silence fell among them all, stunned by what they had seen.

Then the senior SS officer turned to face them to say in a harsh tone, "This a lesson to you all, you who are thinking of escaping. You will be caught and then shot."

Then one of the camp commandant officers gave the order to the camp soldiers for the inmates to be dispersed and moved back towards our huts. Some of them turned to watch while four of the camp soldiers carried the two dead bodies away, ready to be buried. The SS personnel then embarked into their vehicles and the convoy then left the camp. The camp commandant left with his officers and went back into their hut.

Later that day, they found out that the two men were Polish prisoners of war who had escaped a few weeks ago. The two young Polish men were given a full burial with honour, and during the ceremony, the Polish men sung their national anthem with pride in their hearts and souls. Then the camp commandant ordered a full volley of gunfire into the air to mark their respect for the loss of the men.

One inmate turned to David to say that this breaks the articles in the Geneva Convention with regards to the treatment of prisoners. "Those SS are murderers."

David turned to the inmate and said, "Calm down, we need to take this up with our officers to petition the camp commandant over this incident. It is clear that some of the German High Command have little respect for us, and, of course, for the Geneva Convention."

A meeting was held shortly afterwards, and all gave their views on the terrible incident to the panel of senior British, Canadian, Polish, French, Italians, Australians, Asian and American officers. The meeting lasted a couple of hours and was extremely heated and tense. Finally, the officers gave notice to us all that they would meet up with the camp commandant to discuss the situation.

A couple of days had passed when the officers finally met with the camp commandant to discuss the murder of two prisoners. What took place in the meeting was rather heated, according to Major Henderson. He stated that the camp commandant had begged the senior SS officer not to carry out the execution by murdering the two prisoners, but to no avail. The senior SS officer wanted an example to be made to all. The commandant did make it quite clear that they must all bide their time in the camp and not to try to escape. The last thing he wanted was more executions, and stated the next time the SS would take even more drastic measures to punish further escapees and would make many examples to deter them any further, and could decide that the camp be run and headed by a SS unit.

David turned to Major Henderson to say, "But is it our duty to try to escape?"

"Yes," he said. "But we are more unfortunate than most prison camps, as we have a SS garrison five miles away, and the chances are far greater for us to be caught. And also, we do not want to end up having the SS controlling this camp. Look what they have been doing to the Jews in the concentration camp about forty miles away, the SS gain great pleasure from being cruel.

"Believe me, men, I do not like this any more than you. The SS have no time for prisoners and if they had their way, they would be more than happy to shoot us all."

He said further, "For the interests of all, we must unfortunately bide our time. This has been agreed by the commanders of the other allied forces, the risk is too great."

Thereafter, over time Lady especially became preoccupied with playing football and cricket with the men. Lady had a few habits and one in particular was to keep burying their cricket balls, which caused the men to spend a great deal of time trying to find them. Another was as the ball was thrown, Lady would spring up into the air to catch the ball, and then she would run off with it with the cricket team pursuing her frantically. To her, it was fun and a great game.

At other times, she would sit while the game was being played, and bark for the ball to be thrown her way.

As for football, Lady would try and catch the ball partly in her mouth, with the result of puncturing the ball with her sharp teeth and therefore resulting in the ball becoming deflated and the game called off, until the ball was either repaired or replaced.

Happy times, especially for Lady, but the men still loved her. Many a time tug of war was played and you guessed it, Lady was there to join in; the strength of her front legs did help the winning side to win the game.

Several weeks had passed when one of David's comrades early one morning came into the hut, and said, "Please hurry and bring Lady. The young lad who had not long been admitted into the hospital has got worse from the amputation of his leg which was carried out a few days ago, and he has now developed a terrible fever. He does not seem to have the strength to fight it off, and the doctor fears for the worst."

With that, David and Lady hurried out of the hut across the main courtyard and entered the hospital, and walked towards the bed where the young soldier was lying and his fellow comrades were trying to comfort him. The doctor turned to David and whispered in his ear, "I am afraid the young man has not responded to any of the treatments I have given him, all we can do is to make him comfortable."

With that, David sat with the soldier, talking to him, while Lady placed her head on his bed, nudging him. He responded, and started to stoke her. It was a very moving and touching sight, David mopped the sweat from the young soldier's brow for the next half an hour, while Lady rested her head on his chest. Lady then produced tears, and the next thing was the young soldier closed his eyes and fell into a deep sleep. Silence befell all in the room.

The men were so upset as the young man was only seventeen years old. Some men had tears rolling down their face and were also trying to comfort each other. The doctor turned to them. "He is at peace now, and with his Maker, God rest his soul." Lady and David tried to comfort each other over the very sad moment.

That afternoon, the young soldier's body was carried out of the hospital. Soldiers from all forces stood to attention in a mark of respect with the lowering of their heads. Even the German High Command paid their respects at the tragic loss of one so young.

The young lad was then finally laid to rest at the edge of the camp next to where the two Polish soldiers were buried. The British army chaplain led the sermon, prayers were said, and the chaplain gave his blessing to the young soldier. Then the whole congregation started to sing 'Amazing Grace', with one of the Scottish soldiers playing the bagpipes to the tune. Tears rang down David's face, Lady's head was lowered, her ears pointed back, and like so many comrades expressing their emotions over the loss of one of their own. Then a young, black American soldier stepped forward to sing 'Your love keeps lifting me higher and higher', and all joined in this very cheerful and uplifting tune.

The German officers and their soldiers looked on, showing compassion and sadness in their faces, as if it was one of their own men who had died.

A simple headstone was placed with the young man's name on it, with the words:

'To one so young, who has given up so much in the name of freedom, we will always remember you, a brother-in-arms. God bless and sleep tight, you are in Heaven now with the angels.'

A beautiful carving of a dove holding a twig in its beak was at the top of the headstone, and at the bottom his name, his regiment, where he came from and his age.

Then they all started to place some wild flowers and some roses from the trailing rose by his headstone. The German commander then stepped forward, placing a bunch of flowers, then stood up and saluted.

David then said, "Farewell, our brother, may you now find peace in heaven."

For Lady, there were tears in her eyes. David stroked her emotionally. He then crouched down, cuddled Lady and broke down in tears. With that the sun came out and shone onto the headstone, as if God had given his blessing.

Everyday David and Lady would make a special journey to visit the young soldier's grave and the graves of the two Polish soldiers, to tidy up and replace the dead flowers with fresh ones, and then he would kneel down and say a prayer with Lady by his side. "Lady, it is a strange thing we fight wars hoping to bring freedom for those persecuted, only to lose people like these young soldiers. What a price we pay for liberty and freedom," said David as he stroked Lady.

On every parade held, the senior German officer who watched over the parade, always found it a touching sight to see Lady sitting to attention. Once the parade had finished, the camp commandant would come over especially to greet Lady fondly; she, as always, would sit to attention, and give him her paw. He would talk to Lady, and then he would walk away with his other officers back to his hut. Lady certainly made an impression on all with the camp; the saying, 'A man's best friend is his dog', speaks volumes.

During their time at the camp, it was good. The food was reasonable, especially when the food came from the vegetable plot. There were many sports activities, which Lady liked. David always enjoyed growing vegetables and flowers, which was the nearest thing to remembering the good times back home on the farm.

The other entertainment was when some of the men would perform a number of plays, some held outside, but the majority were held in a large hut, to entertain the men as well as a number of German officers and soldiers, who always joined in with a round of applause in appreciation after the show. No doubt, some of the men were very good at acting and some of the plays were comical which always got everyone laughing. Some like Sherlock Holmes mysteries which always went down well with all, to the festive events such as the birth of Christ. Lady had to act the part of a donkey in this; well we'll say no more on this.

But at least the plays took the men's minds off their imprisonment and the war generally.

There was always a Sunday church service which was always well-attended, and then there was the odd Red Cross parcel delivery. The men looked forward to this and were always keen to receive letters from their friends and family back home which gave comfort to us all. Any letters we sent were always vetted by the Germans before they could be sent. For Lady, she always looked forward to receiving any treats from my fellow comrades, the camp commandant, and some of his soldiers who truly loved her, and especially goodies in the Red Cross parcels, a ham bone or even a piece of chocolate, which was exceedingly rare.

Set routines for the men had been laid out by the senior officers of the various allied forces to aim in helping to keep the men's spirits and morals up, also so that they could cope with their time during the duration of the war.

Towards the end of their time in the camp, Lady was starting to disappear in the mornings for short periods of time. It was only by chance when David followed her one day that he found the answer. She had become friends with one of the German soldier's dog, who patrolled around the inside of the camp. A dark black German Shepherd with a bushy tail and long ears called Bruno. She would tease him and get him to play with her. The odd time the soldier would allow his dog off its lead, so he could play with Lady, but always cautious that none of his senior officers were looking.

Eventually, the day came for all, the liberation of the camp by the British troops. Tears of joy rang out of the camp, and David crouched down to Lady and said, "We'll we soon be on our way and back home on the farm with our family." David then finally walked with Lady over to the graves of the young soldiers, placed some fresh flowers, said a prayer, and then said, "Goodbye, you will always be in our hearts. God bless." Then they both walked back to be with his fellow inmates.

On that day the German officers and soldiers dropped their firearms on a pile and surrendered the camp to the British allied forces. They all stood to attention while this event of handing over the camp took place, and next they all got ready to be leave the camp.

Then the German camp commandant walked over to David, knelt down, and pulled out of from his pocket a medal and clipped it onto Lady's collar. Lady then gave him her paw and he hugged her. He said, "I was awarded the Iron Cross for bravery and for serving my country, now I give it to you, Lady, as a thank you for your friendship that you showed me during our time together. God bless you, my faithful friend, I will miss you." He stood up, a tear in eye and he saluted her, and then walked away with the rest of his men.

David was very touched by this gesture of human kindness to a fellow creature. It proves that a number of the German soldiers were after all human beings too in showing kindness to Lady.

The journey took several long tiring days from leaving Stalag 14 prison camp to eventually arriving at the beaches of Normandy. There they finally embarked on troopships to return back to Dover. The journey took a couple of hours on very choppy water. Then at last Lady, David and his fellow comrades disembarked from the troopships at Dover to the smell of the sea breeze, and to the welcoming sounds coming from the local people applauding and cheering them as they marched onto Dover Train Station. Then they eventually embarked onto the train, tired and exhausted from their long journey and they all fell asleep. Lady laid on the floor next to David, as their journey would take some hours.

Finally, they arrived early afternoon at Inkford Railway Station to the further cheering and applauding of the villagers from far and wide. Union Jack bunting was placed across the length and breadth of the railway station, the brass band was playing the Vera Lynn song 'We'll Meet Again'. There were family, friends, lovers; all waiting for the soldiers to disembark from the train.

David turned to Lady. "Well, we are now home at last." Lady wagged her tail in response.

The soldiers disembarked from the carriages to the cheers of joy and excitement from the villagers. Then the soldiers were greeted with hugs of joy by their families, their friends, and even people from far and wide who were also showing their appreciation, for the brave lads had now come back home from the war. They had done their bit for their country and hopefully now had brought some stability back into Europe.

For David and Lady, the whole of the family had turned out to meet them. Mum with tears of joy, hugging and kissing David, his two brothers making a fuss of Lady, and then finally his father came over to David and said, "I have missed you both so much. Welcome home." Then he gave David a big hug and cuddled Lady.

The brass band started again playing various joyful melodies, including 'The Lambert Walk' and 'The White Cliffs of Dover', for all to enjoy and even to dance to. There was plenty of food and drink, which was laid out on long tables for all to enjoy on this special occasion.

But for the Brown Family, all they wanted to do was to climb onto the horse and cart and travel back to the farm to celebrate in their own way the return of David and Lady. But before that, David walked over with Lady to say his farewell to his army comrades, and to say to them, "You will always be welcome up at the farm, but for now, take care, and we hopefully will see you all soon." With that, he hugged his mates and Lady started to brush up to the men with affection.

Then with that, David walked back with Lady, climbed onto the cart, ready to ride off. David sat in the front of the cart with his dad by his side. He patted the young black Shire horse on the back and said, "It's great to see you again, Major." Then his father gave the command for the horse to walk on, Lady seated at the back of the cart, being given a lot of fuss and attention by his mum and David's two brothers.

Eventually, they arrived back at the farm, to the sounds of the various farm animals. They all put the cart and horse into the stable, bedding Major down for the night. Then they all entered the farmhouse to the large spread in the kitchen, which his mum had set out earlier on. There were hams, cheeses, home-made bread, fruit, salads, pies, various cakes, including the fruit cake with the butter cream filling, various fruit cordials, a casket of ale, and the kettle on the hob ready to make the tea, and the smell of the log fire to welcome all.

David's father said, "Great to have you back, son, and you, Lady," and then Dad continued with his joyful speech.

Mum then said. "Come on now, the tea is brewed, let us all sit down and enjoy this feast." With that, she turned to David and gave him a hug. His two brothers, Oliver and Sam, were feeding Lady with some of the ham and pork pies, which she tucked into, smacking her lips with enjoyment.

Next thing, Oliver then said, "My, Lady, you seem to have put on a bit of weight from when we last saw you."

David turned to Lady, stroked her gently on the head and thought to himself, I wonder.

David then, after eating his fill, got up and said, "Well, thank you all. It is great to be back home with my family, we both have missed you so much." Then he kissed his mum and dad goodnight, hugged his two brothers and then went upstairs to his room carrying his rucksack, followed by now, a very sleepy Lady. Dropping the rucksack on the floor, he then fell asleep on the bed with Lady cuddled up to him with her teddy.

David never talked about the war or about his time spent in Stalag 14, as some of the memories of the war were too horrific for him to bear, let alone to confide in others, especially his family. He was so proud of Lady and kept the medal next to a photo of him and Lady. As for the wound to his forehead, he always kept his mop of hair covering it as best he could, so as not to arouse suspicion from his family. Clearly, he did not want anyone to start worrying about his injury. To him, there were more important things in life, like getting adjusted back into civilian life again and helping those he cared for.

As days turned into weeks, David was starting to get back into a normal routine working back on the farm. As for Lady, it was becoming more evident that she was putting on more weight than normal, which started to arouse suspicion with David and his family.

Then one morning, David's mother turned to him and said, "I have been noticing that Lady is starting to go a quiet spot in the sitting room, and has moved some of her bedding there, and that she is also starting to produce milk from her teats. David, I think she is going to have a litter of puppies."

David then said, "During my time in the prison camp, Lady did spend some time with one of the soldier's German Shepherd dog called Bruno."

That was the one and only time David did break his silence about the war to his family.

David's father then replied, "I think it is time we let Mr Johnson the vet take a look at Lady, check her over to see if everything is going to be all right and also find out when the time will be for Lady to give birth. I will pop in to see him, after I have delivered the milk to Mr Franklin the grocer, and also delivered the rest of the milk churns to the railway station to be picked up by the morning freight train to York."

"Dad, don't forgot to pick up the weekly provisions from Mr Franklin," said David's mother.

Then David's father said his goodbyes to the family, got onto the cart and rode off towards the village.

"David, let's try and make Lady as comfortable as possible," said his mum.

"For the time being, I would like to sleep downstairs with Lady, so that I can be there for her," said David.

David then made a fuss of Lady and said, "Now stay here, Lady. I will see you later when I have completed my farm chores." Lady sank down onto her bed, ears back, and with those sad eyes.

"There, there, Lady. Well, you are going to be a mother soon yourself. You need to keep your strength up my love," said David's mum.

David then proceeded towards the farmyard to help his two brothers with the afternoon milking, and then feed and make sure there was fresh bedding down for all of the farm animals.

Mid-afternoon, David's father arrived back from the village with the provisions. David raced over to greet him.

"David, the vet will be here as soon he has done his rounds," said his father, then he headed off to the kitchen carrying the provisions that David's mum had ordered.

David then rode the cart to the stables and fed and watered Major, the Shire horse, and then checked to see that there was fresh bedding in his stable, then finally led him in. "Goodnight, my old friend," he said, stroking him on the head, and then proceeded to finish helping his brothers feed the pigs and chickens.

It was now early evening, and the lads had now finished their chores and headed back to the farmhouse to sit down to their evening meal. They arrived in the kitchen to get freshened up, before then they sat down to beef stew and dumplings. Lady was fast asleep on her blankets in the sitting room. Then all of a sudden came a knock on the door. Lady woke up and rushed over to the door and started barking.

"Hush now, Lady, it can only be the vet," said David.

Dad got up, and proceeded to open the door.

"Hello, Mr Johnson, thank you for coming over," said Dad.

"Well, Mr Brown, let's see. Ah," he said. "Lady, what has happened to you," as he gently led her back towards the sitting room, followed by the family keen to hear the news. He then got Lady to lay down on her blankets and began to check her over.

"Yes, Lady, you are indeed pregnant, and from what I can see, she will soon be giving birth to her puppies. I would say from her size we may be looking at a litter of between six to eight puppies. Lady will know when the time comes, and her instinct will be to lay down and give birth, so a quiet area would best suit her.

"I cannot envisage any complication during the birth, but to play it safe, just give me a call when it is nearing her time to give birth."

"Right, I must make a move, Lady MacCready is expecting me at the old manor house, as she needs me to check over her prized Arab mare, which has gone into labour, to see if all is well."

David's dad then said, "How is Lady MacCready? It must be hard for her these days, living in that big house on her own; to look after and run it."

"Have you not heard? Since the death of her husband after fighting courageously in the First World War, she has now turned most of the manor into a hospital for the injured servicemen. She also regularly helps the doctors and nurses to help bring some comfort to the injured servicemen," said Mr Johnson.

"What a kind gesture. If there is anything we can do to help, please let us know," said Mum.

"Yes, I will convey your kind regards and support to her ladyship. I am sure she would appreciate any help you can give," said Mr Johnson. "Have a good evening all of you, and Lady, I will see you soon," said Mr Johnson, who then stroked her on the head and then with that, he proceeded to take his leave.

"Good night, Mr Johnson, and thank you," said David's dad.

"Well, well, Lady, you certainly are going to have a lot of puppies to look after," said David.

Mum and Dad turned to David and his brothers. "Come on now, let's leave Lady in peace to settle down and finish our tea."

Once tea had finished, Mum cleared the table, Dad sat down to smoke his pipe by the Aga, filling the air with sweet smell of tobacco. The two boys, Oliver and Sam, started to read their comics. Mum eventually sat down to listen to the radio; the programme that night was Agatha Christie's *Murder Most Foul*. David walked off towards the sitting room to make up his bed, and there he sat with Lady, stroking her gently on the head to try and reassure her that all will be well, and then saying to her, "I am so proud of you. You are so special to me, I so love you."

Well, the days passed so quickly. Mr Johnson visited regularly to checks on Lady's progress, and the family, as usual, all tried to keep themselves busy on the farm, patiently waiting for the news that Lady had given birth to her puppies.

It was a cold wet night. David had made up the fire in the sitting room so it was nice and warm for Lady, and he had a feeling that Lady was about nearing her time as she was showing signs of restlessness, pawing at her bedding; she would soon be going into labour. That night once the family had all gone to bed, David settled down near Lady, and tried to comfort her as best he could.

Lady was now starting to wash herself and then trying to make herself comfortable, when the next thing, she finally went into labour. David monitored her progress, making sure she was not going to have any difficulties, and then over the course of the night, Lady finally gave birth, one after another, to eight adorable puppies, David watched over her, while she washed each of the puppies clean, and then she finally settled down to allow them to feed from her nipples. David stroked her gently on the head. "Well done, Lady."

David, now feeling completely exhausted from the late nights, collapsed on the sofa and fell asleep near to Lady and the puppies.

Next morning when the family came down for breakfast, to their surprise they saw Lady grooming her puppies, and David fast asleep.

Dad whispered, "Come now, let's leave them in peace in the sitting room and get ready to have breakfast."

Mum turned to Dad in a quietly spoken voice, "What about David?"

Dad replied, "Let him have a good sleep, it will do him good. And as for Lady, she seems to have everything under control, and what beautiful puppies."

With that, they all headed to the kitchen to settle down to breakfast.

Next thing, David entered the kitchen, yawning. "Sorry, folks. A long night."

With that, he sat down to eat his breakfast.

Then next thing, Lady appeared. Mum got up from the table, "Well, my darling, you must be hungry." She put down a bowl of raw stewing beef and dog biscuits which Lady heartily devoured, licking the bowl clean and then she went to her water bowl to have a good drink.

The family then started to make a fuss of her, before she went back over to the sitting room to her puppies, who were fast asleep with their fat little bellies full of their mother's milk,

Dad turned to the family. "Well, for now let's enjoy the new arrivals to the farm. But David, you know we cannot keep all these puppies. They will have to go when they eventually have been weaned and are old enough to leave Lady in about a few months' time, all being well. I know it is hard, David, but you must also must think of Lady. This has been extremely exhausting for her, and she will have a busy time ahead to look after her puppies. We, of course, will help her as much as possible."

Mum then said, "Can we not at least keep a couple when the time comes?"

Dad replied, "Well okay, but we do need to find good homes for the rest. I suggest we ask around the village."

Next morning after breakfast, David's mum and dad set off to the village to ask around to see if anyone would be interested in the puppies. The response was very good from a number of the villagers, so Dad suggested once the puppies were six months old, the new owners could come to the farm to choose a puppy.

David and his two brothers, as usual, were busy feeding, bedding and milking the cows, making sure also the various farm animals were all right.

David now and then would just pop in to see if Lady was all right with her puppies. He could see that she was a good mother, devoted and very caring towards her puppies.

Time passed, and the puppies eventually had now been weaned, and were starting to eat more and more solid foods and now they were growing at a considerable rate. Each puppy had its own individual personality and some had, by now, various colour markings. But each one was a joy. They loved going outside in the garden to explore, with Lady keeping a watchful eye over them.

They loved the pond, and now and then, one or two would end up in it. Their curiosity was another trait as they liked to try and play with the farm cats who would hiss and run away to hide from them. They also liked to chase the chickens and ducks now and then; in return they would get chased by the geese, and sometimes ended up being pecked. Lady, as always, would sit and watch and would only intervene if she spotted any harm that may come to them.

Over those months, it was a great pleasure to watch them grow into very beautiful young dogs the family loved every minute.

The visitors to the farm, like Mr Johnson the vet, Jim the postman, and the regular visits from the school children, who all loved to come and see Lady with her puppies, but also to walk around the farm to see the various other farm animals. The treat the visitors came for was the warm welcome and homemade cakes. More so for the children was looking forward to a nice slice of homemade fruit cake and a glass of fresh milk, which they all thoroughly enjoyed, before they set back to the village school.

The time finally came.

"Well, Mum, it's time for us to choose the two puppies that we will keep," said Dad to the family.

"It is so difficult to choose, they are all so lovely," said Mum. David's brothers were too interested in playing with them in the garden, while Lady laid down next to David for a well-deserved rest on the sitting room sofa.

"David, what do you think then?" said his dad.

"I agree with Mum, they all are so lovely, and have their own wonderful personalities," said David.

Finally, as difficult as it was for the family, they did choose. A sandy brown and black rather leggy male puppy that they called Troy, and a beige and black marked female puppy that was called Layla.

Next day, Mr Johnson arrived in the morning to check Lady and the puppies over.

"Well," he said, "Lady has done a good job, they all look fit and well, and as for Lady, she is in good health."

"Now from checking the puppies all over, you have three male and five female puppies. Have you all decided on which ones you will keep?" said Mr Johnson.

"The two puppies from the litter, which we will keep are the sandy brown and black male called Troy, and the beige and black female called Layla," said David's dad.

Dad decided a few days ago to purchase two dog collars each with its own metal tag inscribed with the dog's name on, which he then gently put around each of their necks and then fastened securely. They were then put in the sitting room with Lady, while the rest of the puppies were left in the kitchen.

Then Mr Johnson said, "As agreed, I have brought my son Alex along. He is sitting on the cart outside and would very much like to have a puppy." It is quite sad story as Alex was born blind at birth and needs some guidance when he is walking about, the dog would become his eyes. It would then at least give him the chance of being able to go out knowing that he is safe.

"Oliver and Sam, go and help Alex off the cart, and bring him into the kitchen," said David's dad.

The boys then led Alex into the kitchen and he sat down. "I think the best thing is to allow the puppies to move around Alex, and let them sniff at him, and also let him gently touch them as they approach him," said his father.

"Dad, they are so soft and cuddly," said Alex. One particular puppy did stand out from the rest, and she made a real fuss of Alex.

"Dad, may I have this one, please?" said Alex, meaning the one which he held in his arms.

Alex put one hand in his pocket and pulled out a half a crown.

"Thank you, Alex, she is now yours. And what are you going to call her?" said David's dad.

"I will call her Bam," he said.

"That's an unusual name, but a nice one at that, I am sure she will become your friend and companion. She is a very beautiful dog," said David's mum.

"Dad, what is her colour, please?" said Alex.

"She is black, grey and white, and looks a bit like a timber wolf, with a very fluffy tail and long fluffy ears, with such beautiful brown eyes," said his dad.

Mr Johnson then from his coat pocket pulled out a collar and lead, and secured the collar around Bam's neck.

"Here, son. Hold onto her lead tightly." Which he did.

With that, Mr Johnson and his son Alex said their goodbyes and left the kitchen, heading towards their horse and cart.

"Now, now, Mum do not cry. You know it is for the best, and she will be going to a good home, she will give the young lad a lot of love and be able to support him. He, I know, will just love her to bits," said David's dad.

David and his two brothers also looked very sad to see one of the puppies had now left, but they all knew the others would soon be going to their new homes and could only think of the joy that they had given to them during their short time here, but also the love and joy they would give to their new owners.

"Now, boys, let's get the rest of these puppies onto the cart and deliver them to their new owners in the village," said Dad.

Mum said goodbye to them all as they left with tears running down her face. She then turned and headed towards the sitting room to stay with Lady, Troy and Layla.

It was a warm sunny afternoon as the Brown family headed off towards the village with the remaining five puppies. One of the puppies was going to Police Constable Robert Glenny, a tall and stocky man, and well-liked by all. He and his family lived at the end of the village, near the village duck pond. They had chosen a beautiful brindle coloured female puppy. They decided to call her Sasha and she was indeed very soft, affectionate and gentle.

The next puppy was going to the village school mistress, Miss Potter, a quietly spoken lady who showed a real passion for teaching, loved the children in her charge, and was a very keen conservationist. Her house was next to the village school. She had chosen a black male puppy with brown markings on his face, and she decided to call him Zulu; a very alert, friendly and intelligent dog who responded to voice commands by tilting his head from side to side.

The two spinsters well-known for their delicious fruit cake with butter cream filling were Betty and Penny Fortisque, daughters of the late Major Fortisque who fought in the First World War, and who died shortly after from his war wounds. Their mother, unfortunately, died not long after from a broken heart. She was so devoted to her husband, but also adored her daughters very much as well, a very closely knit and loving family. They lived in a large house near the baker's shop. They chose a beige female puppy, and they decided to call her Heidi. She was extremely friendly, liked being made a fuss of and returning her affection. The two ladies then presented Mr Brown, for him and his family, one of their freshly baked fruitcakes filled with that delicious butter cream filling, for them to take home and enjoy.

"Thank you very much, it is very kind of you," said Mr Brown.

Betty and Penny said to them, "Do not forget to give a slice to Lady, you know she loves it."

"We will, and thank you kindly," said David.

Finally, the last two puppies went to Mr Franklin and his family who had the greengrocers and an orchard, and with a large vegetable garden at the back of the property.

The female puppy was black and tan; they decided to call her Sara. She was a very soft and gentle dog, and the male puppy, who was mainly black with very large fluffy ears, they decided to call Max. He was extremely alert, and would tilt his head on hearing voice commands.

Finally, with their farewells, the Brown Family started to head back to the farm.

The two boys were full of tears. "Now, sons, it was the kindest thing to do, we still have two of the puppies. Remember, just think of what joy and happiness these puppies will bring to their new owners. Chin up lads," said Dad.

Once they arrived back at the farm, David's two brothers helped David unharness the horse from the cart, then lead him into his stable, where there was fresh bedding, food and water awaiting him. Then they all proceeded with excitement to the kitchen to see Lady, Troy and Layla who were waiting for them, wagging their tails with excitement.

"Well, Mum, they now are with their new owners, and will, I am sure, settle down well," said Dad.

"The farm is not going to be the same without them," said Mum

"Yes, Mum, but think of the joy they will give to others, as they gave to us. Now cheer up, Mum," said Dad.

With that, Oliver and Sam went out to the back garden with the two puppies, while David went to sit with Lady in the sitting room to quietly sit down together, Lady cuddling up to David.

Dad then said to Mum, "How has Lady reacted, with losing some of her puppies today?"

"She seemed a bit sad at first, but then Troy and Layla started to play with her. That must have taken her mind off the other puppies, they are such lively puppies," said Mum.

Then Dad said. "Come on, boys, let's finish off the farm chores before settling down to hot buttered crumpets, a slice of the delicious fruitcake and a mug of piping hot tea."

Then Mum said, "Right, see you in an hour and I will then have tea ready for you all. And now come on Lady, Troy and Layla, here is your tea, dog biscuits mixed with the left over roast beef in gravy."

All the dogs tucked in, licking their lips afterwards before heading off to the sitting room to sleep it off on the sheepskin rug, all curled up together with their mum Lady.

Well, the evening meal went well, and much was discussed over the kitchen table of that day's events, before all the family finally went upstairs to bed.

Lady, as usual, went to bed with David. Troy and Layla went off to bed with David's two brothers.

Mum then said, "Goodnight and see you all in the morning."

They then replied, "Goodnight, Mum and Dad."

David then started to get undressed when all of a sudden he became dizzy and felt a sharp pain where he was hit by the German bullet. He sat down on the bed and Lady, seeing him in pain, sat next to him, trying to comfort him. He then started rubbing his head, and slowly the pain subsided. David finished putting on his night clothes, then laid down on the bed, and fell asleep with Lady cuddled up next to him.

During the night, calls could be heard coming from David's room.

Mum said, "Dad, should I go and try to comfort him?"

"No, Mum," said Dad. "I think he is having a nasty dream. I will go to see if he is all right now. Mum, why don't you go and make him a nice hot mug of Horlicks which will hopefully help him go to sleep?" said Dad. So Mum went off to the kitchen to make the drink.

Dad went into David's room to find David lying on the bed with his t-shirt and shorts wet from sweat, and Lady slightly wet from lying next to David.

"Come on, son, let's get you into some dry night clothes. Mum is making you some hot Horlicks."

With that, Dad helped David into some dry clothes and proceeded to dry Lady off with a towel, and then helped David back into bed. With that, Lady then hopped back onto the bed and curled up next to David.

"Son, you must have seen such terrible things during your time on active service. This must have triggered you into having a nightmare."

With that, David flung his arms around his dad and burst into tears. Lady then cuddled up to both of them to reassure them.

"Now, now, son, you are safely home with us now. Come on, dry those eyes," said his dad.

Mum then arrived in the bedroom and said, "I have brought us all a nice cup of Horlicks to help us have a good night's sleep."

"Mum, are the two boys awake?" said Dad.

Mum then replied, "No, they are fast asleep with the puppies asleep on their beds. They are out like a light. It seems it would take a lot to wake those sleepy heads." Mum then said, "Here you are, David. Drink this down, it will help you to sleep." With that, Mum kissed David on his cheek. "Now have a good night's sleep."

"Goodnight, son and Lady. See you both in the morning," Dad said.

With that, they left the room, and David then started to fall asleep with Lady cuddled up to him with her teddy.

The following morning, David woke up to feel no pain from his head wound, and so he got washed and dressed and decided to brush off the pain in his head from last night as a one off due to the excitement of being home and the sadness of losing the puppies the day before. The stress must have been too much for him at the time. He then went downstairs with Lady to have breakfast with the family, only to find that already Troy and Layla were playing around in the kitchen with his brothers.

"Now, now, boys, let's finish breakfast. You can then have a quick play with the puppies in the garden before we go to work. David, you stay in and take it easy today," said Dad.

Then the boys and their dad went off to undertake the normal daily chores on the farm.

Mum then said, "First of all, how are you feeling now? Come on, sit down, David. Let me get you and Lady some breakfast. Then after breakfast, have a sit down in the garden, the fresh air will do you good."

"Okay, Mum, I will do that," said David.

As for David's nightmare last night, that was a portent of things to come, as unfortunately he would be experiencing the head pains more regularly as well as those terrible nightmares. All the local doctor could prescribe was plenty of rest and instructions to try to occupy his time, and saying only time can hopefully help in healing.

Now the family, whenever they got a chance while in the village getting the food provisions, would drop in to visit the puppies with their new owners and to see how they were all getting on. It was also an opportunity for them all to spend quality time with the other villagers. This was quite natural in a closely-knit village community, always there looking out for each other. This was very much a caring community, and the community was the heart of the village.

For Lady, however, she undertook many challenges and adventures during her time. Like the rescuing of two fell walkers who became stuck upon the hills as the mist was rolling down. Or the rescuing of the baby lambs who became lost from their mother up in the meadow, and even saving one of the village children who got lost in a bad snowstorm during one hard winter.

But Lady will always be remembered for when she visited the village children at school. They all loved seeing her, but it was also a chance for her to spend some quality time making a fuss of Zulu, who was now starting to grow into a very handsome young dog.

As for Troy and Layla, they would spend as much time together with David's brothers in the garden and also up on the hills. They too had started to grow into very handsome dogs and enjoyed the boys' company whenever possible.

Now and then some of David's old war comrades would meet up either on their own or with their families, especially coming up to the farm to visit him, Lady, and his family. Many a good time they all had together, especially walking around the farm and going up to the hills with the dogs.

David's friends were always welcomed by the true Yorkshire hospitality of a good mug of piping hot tea, homemade cakes, pastries, etc. Mum was known for her baking skills and could always turn her hand to bake something nice for the visitors to enjoy, and always with a warm welcome and smile.

When David used to visit Lady MacCready, Lady used to love playing with the senior gamekeeper's female Labrador called Honey, playing ball and racing around the estate, but also making visits to the soldiers in the hospital set up in the manor.

David, when he had spare time, along with Lady, would visit and help out at the hospital for injured servicemen up at the manor. No job was too small for David to handle, it was always a pleasure for him to help and comfort the injured men. As for Lady, she was always entertaining, and the men, the doctors, and nurses, all loved her for it. It helped bring back something into their lives, especially the soldiers, and this was very rewarding for David to see.

David would also spend some time helping Lady MacCready with her walled garden which also had a large vegetable patch with soft fruits plants and various fruit trees. Lady MacCready loved those fond times with David and especially loved making a fuss of Lady, who had grown very fond of her.

David also spent some time helping to teach the school children in his spare time. He taught them animal husbandry and about the welfare and the care required, and also on how to grow fruit, vegetables and flowers. This the children loved very much.

One time, he even helped to construct a pond in the school grounds with a small wild flower meadow patch for the children to enjoy and to learn more about nature.

David never married, but he would, now and then, visit Lisa Ellen Cook and would go for walks with her and Lady. They all became very good friends over the few years together. Both had mutual interests; the love of the countryside, the pleasure of helping each other out and the observing the wonderful wildlife. Lisa was also a very good cook, very much like David's mother.

Lisa's father, Arthur Cook, ran the local smithy at the end of the village with help from his two sons, Marcus and Jack. It had been a sad event for the family when their mother, Ellen Dorothy Cook, died after suffering a blood clot to the brain a few years ago, not long after Jack was born. So as Lisa was the eldest child, she had to act like a mother to the family, helping to run, clean and cook in the house. Mr Cook was always on hand to help out with his family, and was also very helpful when David's family needed to have the Shire horses reshod every so often, and he also helped when replacing the thick metal hinges on the farm gates and, of course, he was always willing to undertake any other jobs he could turn his hand to help at the farm.

As the years rolled on, David and Lady were by now starting to feel their age. David particularly still suffered some pain from his head wound, and suffer the nightmares now and then, but as usual, would try and keep this away from his family so as not to distress any of them. Only Lady was aware at all times of David's suffering, especially from his war wounds.

They both had resolved to grow old together gracefully. Both had seen the loss of their youth now, but stil their devotion, their love and their bond was forever close.

Then one warm summer's morning, David turned to his father and mother and said, "Today, I would like to be on my own with Lady. I just feel we need to spend some time together."

With that, he gave his mother a kiss on the cheek, and then he hugged his father. Then he said, "Thanks to you both for everything." His brothers were out in the back garden playing with Troy and Layla. He smiled at them through the window, then walked over to the sitting room and into the back garden, went to his brothers and gave them a big hug each, and made a fuss of Troy and Layla.

Then he and Lady left the farm and started walking up the narrow lane, eventually reaching a quiet spot where they both sat down together by a lonely old willow tree next to a cool, bubbling stream. David stroked Lady's head, gave her a kiss, then said, "Thank you, Lady, for being my best friend, for being everything a man could every want. I love you so much, it has been an honour to know you."

Lady then gave him her paw. David cuddled her closely to his chest, stroking her gently, then tears started to roll down David's face, and they both finally fell asleep together. Then from the broken clouds up above, the sun shone down on both of them, like a beam of light, their time had come, and now they were both at last at peace.

An hour had passed since David had left with Lady. The boys were helping their dad on the farm when mum came out of the kitchen and said, "Dad, don't you think David and Lady should have been back home by now? I am concerned. It's not like them."

"Mum, I and the boys will go up to the lane where David always takes Lady for her walks and then see where they are. They are both probably just enjoying the warm sunshine," said Dad. "We will all be back soon, Mum, and so do not worry," said Dad.

Then with that, Dad and the boys set off on their journey up the lane. From a distance, they could see both David and Lady lying cuddled up to each other under a willow tree.

Sam said, "There they are. They must have got tired and decided to have a nap together, Dad."

"Our footsteps would have woken Lady up by now. She would have realised it was us, and then would have woken David up. Something is wrong," said Dad.

Then all three started to race towards David and Lady, their hearts pounding as they ran down the lane towards them.

They finally stopped. Dad bent down to touch David and Lady, who were cold and still. Sam and Oliver stood frozen.

Dad looked up to his two sons now shaking with fear and grief, and with tears rolling down his face, he then said, "I am so sorry. They have both passed away, and are now at peace in God's heaven." Dad was shaken with grief over the loss of his eldest son and his faithful companion, Lady.

Oliver and Sam then bent down to kiss David and Lady on the head, now with tears rolling down their faces, saying, "We are going to miss you both so much, it breaks our hearts."

Dad turned to them and said, "Now both of you stay here, I will go back to the farm and get the horse and cart, and then I will be back soon."

Dad running all the way, eventually arrived back at the farm. Thankfully, he could see Mum was in the kitchen doing her baking, so he then quickly hurried into the stable to harness the horse to the cart and drove off up towards the lane.

Once Dad got there, the three of them then helped to put David's and Lady's bodies onto the back of the cart carefully. They then started to ride back to the farm.

By then, Mum was by the farm gate with Troy and Layla, shouting from that distance, "Is everything all right?" but as they moved nearer and nearer, she could see the tears rolling down their faces.

"Oh no, please God no," Mum said, and then burst into tears.

Dad then said, "Mum. We found then both cuddled up to each other in a dying embrace."

Then Dad, Oliver and Sam got off the cart and ran over towards Mum and they all started to hug each other for comfort, all crying. Layla and Troy sat still, and then silence fell amongst them all on this very sad moment; their world had now turned upside down with grief with the loss of two David and Lady.

Soon the news of David's and Lady's deaths had spread around the village and the surrounding villages. So the villagers would make visits to the farmhouse to pay their respects to the Brown Family for their tragic loss. The commander of David's regiment came to hear of the tragic news, and arrived one day at the farmhouse to pay his respects to the family and to offer to help in any way with the funeral preparations.

He said to David's family, "David was a brave young soldier and comrade, who gave his all. No task was too small for him to undertake. He showed compassion to the sick and injured, a great asset to the army, and will surely be missed by all. As for Lady, she brought such happiness to the soldiers in good and hard times. My wife and I will miss them both so much, I am so proud to have known them both, it has been truly an honour."

Lady MacCready also made a point of visiting the family to convey her sincere regards to the family on this very sad occasion, and also to volunteer to help with funeral preparations.

Lady MacCready said, "David and Lady devoted so much time and energy to help others. I will surely miss both of them, and what a loss to the people who fortunately knew them. It truly has been an honour to have known them both." She then started to wipe the tears from her eyes. She left the farmhouse and was helped onto her pony and trap by her driver.

The local priest, Father Thomas O'Malley, a young man originally from County Cork, softly spoken and kind at heart, always took care and pride towards his parishioners. He made several visits to the Brown Family to help comfort them in their time of need, their grief and also to reassure them that he would assist in anyway with the funeral arrangements.

The day finally came for the funeral, which of course was a very sad affair for the family. It was attended by friends, all the people from the village and also from the nearby villages, and members of the armed force that David and Lady had served with. All knew one thing; that they had lost two very special friends, and that it would not be the same again for any of them.

The coffin containing both David and Lady cuddled up to each other inside, with a single red rose, and also Lady's teddy bear next to her. The coffin, draped with the Union Jack with two red roses on top, rested on a cart with bunches of flowers either side of the coffin. The cart was pulled by two of the farm's Shire horses led by a pall bearer, followed by David's family, friends, the regimental commander and David's old war comrades. The route all the way down to the church was lined by people who had come to show their respect; many tried to hide the tears in their eyes and the grief on their faces.

In front of the possession was a young man carrying a banner with the picture of St Francis and with some of the animals. And also two soldiers, one carrying the Union Jack, and the other carrying the army regimental flag.

The Bishop of York greeted the funeral party at the entrance to the church, with Father O'Malley, and an altar boy carrying the cross. The party then moved through the churchyard towards the church. The coffin was carried by soldiers of David's regiment, to be greeted by soldiers lined up either side of the church footpath, it was truly a very touching moment for all to see. Inside, the church was decorated with flowers. The smell of the roses and

67

incense was quite noticeable by all, the church was already packed full with people, with only enough room for the funeral party to finally take their place inside the church.

Many people had travelled far and wide to pay their respects to David and Lady. The Bishop of York took the service with Father O'Malley. Some of the congregation came up in turn to give a short speech about David's and Lady's lives, including his father, and Lady MacCready. Then the choir sang 'All Things Bright and Beautiful', followed by a speech from the commander of David's regiment, and then a special song, 'If I Had Words', was sung towards the end part of the service.

Many a tears were shed, then finally the funeral procession proceeded outside towards the graveyard. The Bishop of York then said a few words and finally the coffin was gently lowered into the ground. The soldiers instead of giving a gun salute, released white doves into the air as a mark of respect.

On the headstone at the top was carved a dove holding a twig, then underneath the names of David and Lady, with their ages. Then the following words:

'To a loving son and brother who will be truly missed, and to a wonderful faithful companion who gave us joy and happiness. Loved by all, you both have gone, but are not forgotten. It has been an honour to have been blessed and to have known you both, you will always have a place in our hearts. God bless you both.'

Then Father O'Reilly said, "To two such courageous beings, a loving son, brother, friend and his loyal, loving and faithful dog whose duty to king, and country was unprecedented. You will truly be missed, you two comrades of arms; you have reached your final destination now. In heaven with the Holy Father, St Francis and all the saints, Jesus and the Angels of God. God bless you both."

Away from the funeral party, stood an old man and a young woman with a little boy.

The old man turned to the young woman and said, "Did you know David and Lady?"

"Yes," the young woman said. "They were both truly remarkable friends, and it breaks my heart that we will never see them again."

The old man then said, "Is your little boy's father not here?"

"No," she said. "He is sadly dead, and is missed."

She then said, "Did you know David and Lady?"

"Yes," he replied. "I was honoured to know them both while they were in Germany, I too will miss both of them very much."

Once the funeral party had left the grave side, the young woman with her son and the old man then walked to the grave, knelt down and placed some flowers by the headstone, said a few words, then got up and walked their separate ways.

The following morning, David's father decided to walk alone to the lonely tree by the stream, where he and his two sons had found David and Lady. He then knelt down, placing some flowers by the base of the tree. He said a prayer, then sung 'I Always Love You' with a tear in his eye, then he got up to start to walk away.

Then as he did, he felt a hand touch his shoulder. He turned towards the tree and there he saw the vision of his son, David, and Lady looking at him. David smiling, Lady, her head tilted. Tears started rolling down his father's cheeks. He then said, "I am truly going to miss you both, it breaks my heart that you both are no longer part of our lives."

"Father, we will always be with you and the family. God bless you," said David, Lady barked holding her paw up, then the vision of them both started to fade away.

David's dad then started to walk back down the lane towards the farmhouse to be with his family, stunned at what he had seen.

The days passed by, the villagers as usual rallied round to help the family as best they could, with the comfort, the support, and the love of friendship, in the Brown Family hour of need.

A couple of weeks then passed, when one cold wet October morning, there was a knock at the kitchen door. Dad went over to open the door. There stood Lady MacCready and her driver, carrying a large box.

"Good morning, Lady MacCready. Please do come in," said Mr Brown.

With that, the family stood up from the kitchen table to greet her and her driver, the two dogs Layla and Troy raced in from the sitting room, curious to know what was in the box, which was by now showing some movement.
Mrs Brown then said, "Would you both like to sit by the warm fire, take some refreshment?"

"Thank you kindly, no. We have some pressing business to discuss with you all. Now, young Troy, you have certainly shown an interest in my female German Shepherd, Poppy, on many occasion. As a result..." said Lady MacCready.

She then paused. "We would like, as a token of our appreciation, for the kindness your family has shown us, and the villagers, in particular David and Lady, to present you with this gift," said Lady MacCready.

The driver then placed the box on the floor, and then opened it to reveal a black and tan female German Shepherd puppy.

"By the way, her name is Lady. We hope you will treasure her. Now, Lady, live up to your name. We must now leave you all, thank you, Oh, before I forget there is a further surprise that will bring happiness back into your lives, but for now you will have to wait and see," said Lady MacCready.

"Thank you, Lady MacCready," said Mr Brown.

As they left the kitchen, the family waved goodbye, and returned to the kitchen, to see Troy and Layla playing with their new friend. Tears of joy rolled down the family's faces.

"Dad, she looks just like Lady," said Mum.

"Yes, and we know who the father is, don't we Troy," said Dad. Troy sat wagging his tail, and tilting his head, and Layla started chasing Lady around the kitchen table.

Mum turned to Dad and said, "I wonder what Lady MacCready meant by we would receive a further surprise?"

The day finally came as Lady MacCready had said; the family was sitting around the kitchen table having their evening meal when there was a knock on the kitchen door. The dogs started barking.

"Hush now, let see who is at the door."

Mr Brown opened the door to see Mr Cook, the blacksmith, with his daughter, Lisa, holding the hand of a little boy.

"Do come in and sit down. What can we do for you?" said Mr Brown.

Mrs Brown offered them refreshments, and then they all sat down around the kitchen table, while the little boy sat making a fuss of the dogs.

Mr Cook then said, "You probably know that your son, David, had been seeing my daughter, Lisa, for the last few years, and the result is, with joy in my heart, that I am proud to say, may I now introduce you all to you my grandson, David Christopher Brown."

Tears started to roll down the Brown Family's eyes. Their son had left them a very special gift for them to treasure for years to come.

They all talked for many hours that evening, and over time, got to spend much time together. Lisa and young David eventually lived up at the farm with the dogs. David loved the dogs, but had a very special affection for Lady. The Cook and Brown families united into one big happy family and many happy years followed.

Many a time Dad, Mum, David's two brothers, Lisa, Lisa's dad, and young David would walk with Troy, Layla and young Lady up the lane to place flowers under the lonely willow tree next to the flowing stream.

As to what happened to young David and Lady, that is another story.

The ending to this story is happiness will always triumph over sadness. Where there are tears, there will be joy, good will always prevail over evil, and that you must always show kindness, love, compassion, help and understanding to your fellow human beings, and to the animals that we share our wonderful world with.

In honour of their bravery to their country, their love for their community, and to their unconditional love for each other, the surrounding villages commissioned a statute of David and Lady to be placed in the middle of their village for all to see, and for all to remember what courage and devotion to duty they gave, and also to commemorate the many servicemen and their fellow animals who died in the world wars.

Thereafter on each anniversary of the First and Second World War, wreaths of red poppies each containing some blue poppies, would be laid by the statute of David and Lady. At the bottom of the statute is a large plaque with the names of all the brave soldiers from the village who died in those wars.

The red poppy is to symbolise the loss of the soldiers who died, and the blue poppy to mark a very special dog and the other animals who gave up their lives in the service for king and country.

We must never forget the people that gave up their lives in those wars, to allow us to have freedom of speech, and democracy, but also so that the future generations can live in peace. But we should also show our thanks, appreciation, especially to the animals, which played such a special part in those wars, those unsung heroes.

I dedicate this stories to those special animals that have played a part in my life:

Especially to Layla who passed away on 24th September 2015.

Troy, Zulu, Sasha, Bam, Max, Sara, the German Shepherds. To Heidi and Honey the Labradors, to Poppy and Sasha the Boxers, to Bruno the Rottweiller.

To Libby, Tao, Laura, Pickwick, Kim, Spectra, Sasha, and Lowyra the Siamese cats, to Kip, Tigger, Tabs, Fluff, Barnaby, Chi Chi the domestic cats.

To Billy the cockatiel, to the silkie hens, the rabbits, guinea pigs, and all the other animals I have had the pleasure of keeping, God bless them all.

To my mum, Lisa (to my dad, she will always be his very special lady), my dad, David. To my special nephew, Oliver, who will always be a very special son. Nan and Granddad Cook, Nan and Granddad Brown, Phyllis and Mollie, Lorna, Richard, Paul, Kathy, Nicky, Kevin, Keith,

Paul, Ray, Mr and Mrs Harbour, Aunty Glenny. To my present and past work colleagues, friends, fellow conservationists, thank you, and God bless you all.

Above all, to the special characters in this story, David and Lady. God bless you both.

This world would not be a nice place if I had not had the privilege of meeting these people, and having the friendship, and unconditional love from those beautiful animals, God bless you all.

Also with thanks to BBONT, RSPCB, RSPCA, PDSA, Greenpeace, Help for Heroes/war veteran charities, Cancer Research, The Roman Catholic church priests and friends, and above all his Holiness Pope Francis, Oxfordshire Animal Sanctuary, Hart Veterinary Practice, and the National Society for the Preventions to Cruelty to Children.

APPLICATION FOR REGISTRATION
OF AN ORCHID HYBRID

PAYMENT MUST ACCOMPANY THE APPLICATION

P: ___ T: ___ *Registrar's use only*

(Before filling in this form please consult the notes overleaf.
Use block capitals or typescript.)

Your ref/seedling no.*

I enclose a cheque* for £10.00* / US$16.50*
OR
Debit £10.00 from my American Express* / Visa* / Mastercard* / Diners* credit card   Expiry date

No: | | | | | | | | | | | | | | | |

delete as applicable (US dollar cheques only accepted for two or more registrations)

GREX	GENUS -	CYMBIDIUM
	GREX EPITHET (1ST CHOICE) -	LAYLA - TROY
	GREX EPITHET (2ND CHOICE) -	

TWO CHOICES **MUST** BE GIVEN

DATE OF MAKING CROSS (ie. pollination)	FEB · 2012	DATE OF FIRST FLOWERING	APRIL -2016

see Note 6 overleaf

BRIEF DESCRIPTION OF FIRST FLOWERS - see overleaf to continue

UPRIGHT STEM 3" WHite/cream FLoWERS

PARENTS	SEED ♀		POLLEN ♂
GENUS:	CYMBIDIUM	GENUS:	CYMBIDIUM
EPITHET:	SHOWGIRL	EPITHET:	SUSSEX DAWN
	Specific or Grex Epithet		*Specific or Grex Epithet*
EPITHET:		EPITHET:	
	Varietal or Cultivar Epithet (Optional)		*Varietal or Cultivar Epithet (Optional)*

APPLICANT	TITLE:	MR	FORENAMES:	PETER ANTHONY
SURNAME:	OR TRADING NAME:	ORCHIDS BY PETER WHITE		
ADDRESS:	61 STANWELL LEA,			
	MIDDLETON CHENEY, BANBURY			
POSTCODE:	OX17 2RF	COUNTRY:	UK	
FAX/PHONE *(optional)*	01295- 712159	E-MAIL *(optional)*	Peter.orchid@sky.com	

I do / do not* authorise the disclosure of parental cultivar epithets *delete as appropriate*

Applicant's declaration regarding originator

Either (1) I am the Originator as defined in Note 5 overleaf .... ☑
Or (2) The Originator is unknown as explained by me overleaf .... ☐
Or (3) The Originator's name and address is:
ORCHIDS BY PETER WHITE ☐

Colour photograph enclosed? Yes/No* *delete as appropriate (see Note 7 overleaf)*

and (a) has given permission for this application .... ☑
or (b) is no longer extant, has no living spouse and no assignee is known to me ...... ☐
or (c) has not replied to any written request for permission
as sent to him on .... *(date - over 3 months ago)* ☐

ONE BOX ABOVE MUST BE TICKED

I certify to the best of my knowledge and belief the particulars and declaration given above are correct. I agree to my personal details being kept on record.

Signature of applicant ...... P. A. White .... Date ... APRIL - 2016 ......

NO APPLICATION CAN BE ACCEPTED UNLESS ALL THE DECLARATIONS ABOVE ARE COMPLETED

Application for naming an orchid as Layla-Troy

Cymbidium Layla Troy

Genus	*Cymbidium*
Epithet	Layla Troy
Synonym Flag	This is not a synonym
Registrant Name	P.White
Originator Name	P.White
Date of registration	24/11/2016

	Seed parent	Pollen parent
Genus	*Cymbidium*	*Cymbidium*
Epithet	Showgirl	Sussex Dawn

Application for naming an orchid as Layla-Troy (continued)

Layla-Troy Orchid

Pet dog lives on in name of orchid

Rare plant named after Layla who was treated with it for cancer by her owner

Naomi Herring
nherring@trap.com

A PET owner in Bicester hopes to create a legacy for his dog after she underwent alternative herbal cancer treatment.

Chris Hayes-Brown, owner of 13-year-old German Shepherd Layla who passed away last September, opted to treat her cancer with a plant from his garden.

Mr Hayes-Brown researched herbal treatments for Layla when she developed cancer in her jaw and said he was told she may only live a few weeks.

But after researching herbal alternatives to chemotherapy he discovered a rare orchid which is used elsewhere in world for treatment.

It uses a form of Bletilla orchid which Mr Hayes-Brown grows and he asked the vets if they could try it.

He said: "The method used the plant's tuber crushed up and injected into the tumour in Layla's

Chris Hayes-Brown hopes to create a lasting legacy for his dog Layla after her battle

mouth. I noticed that Layla responded well and felt the orchid was attacking the cancer, causing parts to turn black and die away.

"The cancer was trying to fight back, but the orchid seemed to be keeping it to the side of the jaw. It gave her a breath of new life."

Unfortunately Layla had to be put to sleep after the tumour made her jaw too weak, but Mr

Hayes-Brown said she managed to live an extra 14 weeks.

He added: "Over the years Layla touched the hearts of many and was such a devoted dog, we are proud and honoured to have known her."

Mr Hayes-Brown has been in touch with orchid enthusiasts who he says have agreed to name a Cymbidium orchid "Layla Troy" in her honour, and it is registered with the RHS.

He hopes more will be named to continue the lasting legacy including Bletilla, Phaius and Cattleya orchids.

The vet who treated Layla, who wanted to remain anonymous, said: "She was a lovely dog with a great personality and I knew Chris raises her dreadfully.

"There was some information available suggesting the orchid may have some anti-cancer properties, though we could find no evidence of placebo-controlled clinical trials.

"Given that Layla had nothing to lose and we found no reports of toxicity we agreed that Chris could try the herbal supplement.

"Chris believes that the herbal supplement from the Bletilla orchid helped Layla fight her cancer. Maybe it did help her in some way, though personally I am sceptical."

Layla, German Shepherd

Troy, German Shepherd

Zulu

Sasha

Bam (above and below)- Silver Sable

Heidi

Sara

Max (left) and Sara (right)

Honey- Labrador Retriever

Bramley- wild rabbit

Libby- Lilac Point Siamese